Sherlock Holmes

ARTHUR CONAN DOYLE

Adapted by Trevor Millum

PACIFIC
L E A R N I N G

© 2001 Pacific Learning
© 2000 Adapted by **Trevor Millum**
Written by **Arthur Conan Doyle**
Cover illustration by **David Axtell**
Inside illustrations by **Shirley Bellwood**
US Edit by **Rebecca Weber McEwen**

This Americanized Edition of *Stories of Sherlock
Holmes,* originally published in English in 2000, is
published by arrangement with Oxford University
Press.

05 04 03 02 01
10 9 8 7 6 5 4 3 2 1

Published by
  Pacific Learning
  P.O. Box 2723
  Huntington Beach, CA 92647-0723
  www.pacificlearning.com

ISBN: 1-59055-086-2

PL-7608

Contents

The Boscombe Valley Mystery

CHAPTER 1

An Ordinary Crime?

My name is Dr. Watson and I have the good fortune to be the friend and companion of Sherlock Holmes. I try to keep a record of the cases he has solved. I have been with him many times when he has solved cases with just a few clues and his powerful brain.

One such case was the Boscombe Valley Mystery. I knew nothing about it until I received a telegram early one morning at home. It was from Holmes, asking me to go with him to western England. My wants are few and simple so I swiftly packed a case, said farewell to my wife, and was at Paddington Railway Station in less than an hour.

Holmes was already there. He was instantly recognizable: tall and gaunt – and dressed in his long gray cloak and deerstalker hat.

"It's good of you to come, Watson."

We had the carriage to ourselves and Holmes spent the time reading a huge pile of newspapers. Now and then he stopped to make notes and think. Finally, he tossed the papers onto the luggage rack.

"What do you know of the case?" he asked.

"Nothing. I haven't seen a paper for days."

"Hmm," Holmes said. "It's one of those simple cases that are so extremely difficult."

"What do you mean?"

"The more ordinary a crime seems to be, the more difficult it is to see the solution. It is the unusual that makes things easy!"

"What kind of crime is this?" I asked.

"Murder, Watson. A serious case has already been made against the son of the murdered man. It happened in Boscombe Valley, near Hereford, where Mr. John Turner owns a great deal of land. He came back from Australia a few years ago and settled here."

"I take it he made his fortune in Australia?"

"Enough to buy several farms. One he rents out to another Australian named Mr. Charles

McCarthy. McCarthy has an eighteen-year-old son named James."

"Do any of them have wives?" I asked.

"Neither of the wives is still living, but Turner has one daughter near James's age."

"What's the story behind the murder?"

"It seems that last Monday, McCarthy left his house at Hatherley at about three in the afternoon. He walked down to Boscombe Pool, a small lake at the end of Boscombe Valley. He told his servant that he had an appointment at three o'clock. He never came back alive.

"Two people saw McCarthy walking toward the pool, and both say he was alone. The gamekeeper says that a few minutes later James McCarthy went the same way, carrying a gun. He thought the son was following his father."

"Was the father shot?" I asked.

"Oh no," Holmes replied. "Please wait. There was another witness. Patience Moran, the daughter of the lodge-keeper on the Boscombe Estate, was picking flowers in the woods. She says that she saw James and his father having a violent quarrel. She heard

Charles McCarthy using strong language with his son and she saw the son raise his hand as if to strike his father."

Holmes continued, "She ran away and told her mother. Almost as soon as she had finished telling her story, James McCarthy ran up and said he had found his father dead. They followed him and found the body by the side of the pool. The head had been beaten in by blows from some heavy and blunt weapon."

"Such as the butt-end of a gun?" I asked.

"Exactly. Anyway, James McCarthy was arrested and charged with his father's murder. It doesn't look good for the young man."

"Has he said anything?"

"Indeed he has, and it makes an interesting case. According to James McCarthy, he was in Bristol for three days. He came back to find that his father was out. He set out to hunt rabbits at the other side of Boscombe Pool. About a hundred yards from the pool, he heard a cry of 'Cooee!' which was the usual signal between him and his father.

"His father was surprised to see him. For some reason, an argument took place and James walked off. He had not gone far when he heard a dreadful cry.

"According to his story, he returned and found his father dying. He held him in his arms but he could do nothing. He then ran off to the lodge-keeper's for help."

"Is there nothing else to go on?" I asked.

"Two things that could be important," Holmes said. "James heard his father speak before he died. He said he spoke about a rat."

"A rat!"

"Precisely, my dear Watson. The other matter was the subject of the quarrel."

"Which was?"

"James McCarthy refused to tell the police what they quarreled about."

"Refused?"

"Quite so." Holmes looked up at me, raised his eyebrow, and smiled. "You see why I am interested, Watson? This is not such a simple case as they would have us believe."

CHAPTER 2

A Blow from Behind

We arrived at the Hereford Arms at half past four. We were sipping our tea when the door burst open and in rushed one of the loveliest young women I have ever seen.

"Oh, Mr. Holmes!" she cried. "I am so glad you've come. James didn't do it. We've known each other all our lives – he wouldn't hurt a fly."

"You may rely on my doing all that I can," Holmes replied, deducing correctly that the lady was Mr. Turner's daughter, Alice.

"James didn't do it," she repeated. "And that quarrel with his father – I am sure he refused to speak of it because it concerned me. You see, Mr. McCarthy wanted James to marry me. We've always cared for one another – but James is so young – and he is not willing to commit himself to such a step..." She blushed and I decided that she would not object to marrying him, however.

"Thank you," Holmes said. "Do you think I could see your father tomorrow?"

"I am afraid the doctor won't allow it."

"The doctor?"

"Haven't you heard? Poor Father has not been strong for years, and this has made him quite ill. He was so strong once – when he was in Australia. Mr. McCarthy was the only man who knew him in those days."

"Really?" Holmes said. "That is interesting. Thank you, Miss Turner. You're a great help."

She smiled gratefully. "I must go home now. Father misses me so, if I leave him." She hurried from the room as impulsively as she had entered.

Holmes decided to set off for Hereford immediately to see James McCarthy, and while he was away I pondered the details of the murder. The local paper had the full report, including a description of the injuries. The bones on the left side of the skull, at the back, had been shattered by a heavy blow.

I thought about what this meant. Such a blow would have been struck from behind, which isn't normal in a face-to-face argument. Then there was the matter of the man's dying words. "A rat..." What could it mean?

Holmes returned late without much more information. He had found out, though, the truth about James' feelings toward Miss Turner.

"He is madly in love with her," Holmes remarked.

"Then why the argument with his father?"

"Because, Watson, he is already married."

"Great heavens! He's practically still a boy!"

"He was even more of a boy when he met up with a waitress in Bristol. He married her secretly over a year ago."

"So he is being scolded for not doing what he would love to do! How maddening!"

"Quite so. However, it seems his young wife threw him over when she found out he was in trouble. She told him she is already married to a man who is in jail, so there is no tie between them. Unfortunately, this doesn't make up for being charged with murder."

"But if he is innocent, who did it?"

"Let me draw your attention to two things, Watson. First, the murdered man had an appointment with someone. That person could not have been his son. His son was away and he didn't know when he was returning.

"The second thing is that the murdered man was heard to cry 'Cooee!' before he knew his son was anywhere near. The case depends upon such things!"

CHAPTER 3

The Scene of the Crime

The following morning we set off for Hatherley Farm and the Boscombe Pool. As the carriage bounced down the country lanes, Holmes turned to me.

"There is one other interesting fact, Watson. Mr. McCarthy lived at his farm rent free."

"That's very generous of Mr. Turner," I replied. "But then, they were friends back in Australia."

"Doesn't it seem odd, though? McCarthy, who had so little money, talked confidently of marrying his son to Turner's daughter – and I have found that Turner himself was against it."

It did seem odd, but I could deduce nothing from it. We soon arrived at Hatherley farm, with a comfortable looking two-story house. The maid, at my friend's request, showed us the boots Mr. McCarthy had been wearing. She also found a pair of his son's boots.

Holmes measured them all very carefully and then set off to the pool. It was marshy ground and there were marks of many feet on the path and on the short grass beside it.

"How simple it would have been," Holmes exclaimed, "if I'd been here before they came in like a herd of buffalo. Many of the important tracks have been ruined."

He peered at the ground, then cried, "Aha! Here are three separate tracks of the same feet."

He took out a magnifying glass and lay down to get a better view.

"These are young McCarthy's feet. Twice he was walking and once he ran swiftly. The soles are deeply marked but the heels are hardly visible. That bears out his story. Here are the father's feet as he paced up and down. Ha! What have we here? Someone else was walking on tip-toes. Tip-toes! Square, too – unusual boots. Now, where did they come from?"

Holmes paced up and down, sometimes losing and sometimes finding the trail. He

stopped at the edge of the woods and next to a great beech tree he lay down again. He stayed there a long time, turning over leaves and dry twigs. He picked up a jagged stone and examined it carefully. Then he got up and followed a path through the woods that led to the main road, where he stopped.

He showed me the stone. "If I am not mistaken, it is the murder weapon," he said.

He did not sound as if he expected to be mistaken but I had to ask, "How can you tell? There are no marks on it."

"The grass was growing under it so it had only been there a few days. It matches the injuries and there is no sign of another weapon."

"What about the murderer?"

"The murderer is a tall, left-handed man. He limps with his right leg and wears thick-soled shooting boots. He smokes Indian cigars, uses a cigar holder, and carries a blunt pocketknife. There are several other clues, but these may be enough to aid us in our search."

Holmes was silent for a long time and we did not speak again until we were back at the Hereford Arms.

CHAPTER 4

A Rat!

After lunch, Holmes sat staring into space. Then he turned to me.

"I don't know quite what to do, Watson. I would appreciate your advice. Let me explain."

"Please do so."

"Let us first presume that what young James said was true."

"Which part in particular?"

"Actually, there are two main points to consider. One I mentioned earlier – his father calling 'Cooee' *before* seeing him. The other was McCarthy's dying words about a rat."

"What of this Cooee, then?"

"It could not have been meant for his son. As far as McCarthy knew, his son was in Bristol. The Cooee was meant to call the person he was meeting, and it is an Australian greeting. Therefore, he was expecting to meet someone from Australia."

I nodded. "And the rat?"

Holmes took out a folded paper from his pocket. "This is a map of the colony of Victoria in Australia. I had it sent over this morning." He put his hand over part of the map. "What do you read?"

"ARAT," I said.

"And now?" He raised his hand so I could see the whole word.

"BALLARAT," I said softly.

"Exactly. That was what McCarthy said. His son only heard the last part. He was trying to name his murderer. 'So-and-so of Ballarat.'"

"That's amazing!"

"It's obvious. Now we're looking for a tall Australian who is at home enough in the district to find his way through the estate."

"You deduced his height from the length of his stride – but what about his lameness?"

"The mark of his right foot was always less clear than his left. He put less weight on it. Why? Because he limped."

"What about his left-handedness?"

"You read the official police report about the injury. A blow struck from behind yet from the left side. Surely a left-handed man? He stood behind the tree during the argument between James and his father. He even smoked there – I found the ash of a cigar and the cigar stump in the moss where he'd thrown it. The tip of the cigar was cut off in a ragged fashion, so I deduced a blunt penknife."

"I see where this all points. The murderer must be..."

"Mr. John Turner!" cried a voice. It was the hotel waiter, opening the door. He showed a visitor into the room.

The man who entered was a strange and impressive figure.

He had a slow limping step, but his craggy face and huge arms and legs gave an impression of strength of body and character. His face was white and his lips tinged with blue. As a doctor I could see that he was a very ill man.

"Please take a seat," Holmes said. "Did you receive my note?"

"Yes, that's why I'm here. You said you wished to see me here to avoid scandal."

"I thought people would talk if I came to your estate."

"Why did you wish to see me?" the man asked wearily.

"I know all about McCarthy," Holmes said.

The old man sunk his face in his hands. "I didn't know what to do!" he cried. "I would have spoken out, though. I would not have let that young man come to harm."

"I'm glad to hear it," Holmes said gravely.

"I would have explained already, but my dear daughter... It will break her heart when she sees me arrested."

"It may not come to that," Holmes said.

"What?"

"I am no police officer. Your daughter is the one who invited me here and I am acting in her interests. The important thing is to clear the name of young McCarthy."

"I am a dying man," Turner said. "The doctor says I have only a month. Even so, I would still rather die under my own roof than in jail."

"Just tell us the truth while I jot down the facts. You will sign it with Watson as a witness. If the case goes against young McCarthy I shall use your confession. You may be assured I shall not use it unless it is absolutely needed."

"Thank you," the old man said. "I doubt I shall live until the trial, but I would still like to spare Alice the shock. I will tell you all. It will not take long."

CHAPTER 5

A Riddle Answered

"Old McCarthy was a monster. His grip has been upon me for nearly twenty years. He has destroyed my life," Turner said.

"The story began nearly thirty years ago at the Australian gold mines. I was young and hot-blooded, but I had no luck with my search for gold. I made some bad decisions, and I became a highway robber. There were six of us and we had a wild, free life. Black Jack of Ballarat was the name I took.

"One day a gold convoy was traveling from Ballarat to Melbourne. We attacked it and in the fight three of our boys were killed before we got the loot. McCarthy was the driver.

"We got away with the gold and became wealthy men. Later, I made my way to England. I wanted to settle down and do some good with my money, to make up for how I'd earned it. I married and, though my wife died young, she left me my darling daughter Alice.

"I did my best to lead a good life. All was going well until I ran into McCarthy in Regent Street, up in London. He had hardly a coat on his back or a boot to his foot.

"'Well, well, Jack!' he said. 'My son and I have just become your family. You can take care of us. If you don't, this is a law-abiding country – and there's always the police...'

"Well, McCarthy and son came down here and there was no shaking them off. They lived rent free at Hatherley on my best land. There was no rest. No peace.

"It grew worse as Alice grew up. He saw that I was more afraid of her knowing my past than I was about the police. Whatever he wanted, I gave without question. From me he had land, money, houses – until at last he asked what I could not give. He asked for Alice.

"He had the awful idea that his son should marry my girl so when I died his family could take the whole property.

"But I would not do it. I do not dislike the lad, but McCarthy blood is in him and that is enough. McCarthy threatened me. I dared him to do his worst. Finally, we agreed to meet at the pool, which is midway between our houses, to talk it out.

"I went down there and heard him talking with his son. He was urging his son to marry Alice with no regard for what she might feel. It drove me mad to think that I and all that I held most dear should be in the power of such a man! I had to silence his foul tongue! I did it, Mr. Holmes. I struck him down with all the strength I still have. And that is the truth."

"It is not for me to judge you," Holmes said as Turner signed the statement. "You must make your peace with yourself."

"Farewell, then," the old man said. "Your own deathbeds, when they come, will be the easier for the thought of the ease you gave to mine." He stumbled slowly from the room.

"I'll never get used to this," Holmes said after a long silence. "Why does fate play such tricks with poor helpless worms?"

James McCarthy was acquitted at the trial, mainly because of the evidence presented by Holmes in his defense. Old Mr. Turner lived another seven months. There is now every chance that James and Alice may yet live happily together – in ignorance of the cloud that rests upon their past.

The Adventure of the Blue Carbuncle

CHAPTER 1

A Goose and a Bowler Hat

I called on my friend Sherlock Holmes soon after Christmas. He greeted me warmly and we sat by his cheery fire. It was frosty outside and I was glad of the warmth. As we sat down, he pointed to an old bowler hat.

"Now this is an interesting trophy, Watson."

"To you, Holmes, I am sure it is."

"Peterson found it."

I knew Peterson. He was the doorman for the block of apartments where Holmes lived.

Holmes went on. "Peterson was going home late one night when he noticed a tall man in front of him, carrying a goose – no doubt for his Christmas meal. As this man reached the corner of Goodge Street, he bumped into some rough types coming in the opposite direction.

As they started to surround him, the man raised his walking stick to defend himself and smashed a pane of glass behind him.

"At this point Peterson came along and the roughs ran off. In the dark his uniform probably made him look like a policeman. The tall man ran off too, perhaps thinking that he would be in trouble for breaking the window. Anyway, in the fracas he left behind the goose and the hat, which Peterson brought to me. He knows how I like even a small mystery."

"So the poor fellow lost his dinner!" I said.

"It would seem so. Inside the hat there was a label, with the name 'Mr. Henry Baker' – but there are hundreds of people with that name in London. I told Peterson to take the goose himself but I kept the hat." Holmes offered it to me. "See what you can make of it," he said.

I looked at the battered object. The red silk lining was dirty and there were holes for a hat securer. The hat was very dusty and there were patches where the black had faded. Some of these had been smeared with ink.

"I can deduce nothing," I said.

Holmes took the hat and gazed at it in the peculiar fashion which I had seen so many times before. He then said, "The owner used to be well-off, but is no more. He used to think ahead but is now more careless. He is out of shape, is probably middle-aged, and his house does not have electricity. He has gray hair, recently cut, on which he uses lime-cream. Oh, and I doubt that his wife cares for him as much as she used to."

"Heavens, Holmes, how can you possibly know all that?" I cried.

"This hat is three years old; this brim style was in fashion then. It is of good quality – look at the lining. So, he bought an expensive hat three years ago but now it is old."

"He still wears it, though," I said.

"Exactly, which is why I suspect he has fallen on hard times. He was more careful than he is now. See the marks for the hat securer? The elastic fell off and he did not replace it. He has become careless. The ink marks, however, show that he still makes some effort, as he is trying to hide the fade marks on the outside."

"What about the other details?" I asked.

"If you look closely you will see the small gray hair ends showing a recent haircut; and you will catch the smell of lime-cream. There are marks of moisture – almost certainly sweat. Anyone who perspires so much is not fit."

"But his wife? You said..."

"Ah, yes. That's just a guess, Watson. The hat has not been brushed for weeks. What loving wife would allow her husband to go out like that? When I see you in such a hat I shall know that your wife no longer cares for you!"

I smiled. "Well, perhaps. Now what about the electricity – or lack of it?"

"There are a number of tallow stains on the hat. This chap uses candles in his home."

I was amused. "Very interesting, Holmes. What a pity no crime has been committed."

As if on cue, the door burst open. It was Peterson.

"Mr. Holmes! The goose, sir!" he gasped.

"Has it come to life and flown away?" Holmes asked.

"Sir, look what my wife found inside of it."
He held out his hand. There in his palm was a
jewel, a blue stone that shone like a little light.

"By Jove!" Holmes exclaimed. "It is the blue
carbuncle!"

"The Countess of Morcar's jewel?" I cried.
"The one stolen from Hotel Cosmopolitan?"

"Exactly that," said Holmes. "It was taken
just a few days ago. John Horner, a plumber,
is accused of the crime." He picked up a
newspaper and found what he was seeking.

"According to the news reports, Horner was
asked to do some minor work in the Countess
of Morcar's dressing room. James Ryder, a
porter, brought him to the room to do the
work but was then called away for a while.
When he came back he found that the bureau
had been forced open. The jewel case was open
and it was empty. Ryder gave the alarm and
that evening Horner was arrested."

"What did Horner have to say?" I asked.

"He said he was innocent. However, he has
a previous conviction for robbery. The jewel
was not found…"

"Until now!"

"Indeed, Watson. Now let us think how far we have got with this little mystery. Here is the jewel. The jewel came from the goose and the goose came from a Mr. Henry Baker. So we must find Mr. Baker, the owner of the hat!"

I nodded.

"The easiest way may be to place an advertisement in today's newspapers." He turned to Peterson. "I wonder if you would be so kind..." Holmes spent a few moments drafting a short notice.

"This will do. 'Found at the corner of Goodge Street, a goose and a black bowler hat. Mr. Henry Baker may have both by applying at 6:30 tomorrow at 221B Baker Street.'"

CHAPTER 2

Mr. Baker Arrives

The ad was placed in several evening papers. Peterson purchased a goose, similar to the one he and his family had eaten. Just before 6:30 the next day Holmes and I waited to see if the owner of the goose would turn up.

At 6:35 there was a knock at the door. A tall man stood there, dressed in a shabby overcoat.

"Mr. Henry Baker, I presume," Holmes said. "I believe this is yours." He pointed to the hat.

"Yes, sir. That is my hat, without a doubt."

"Good. I'm afraid we had to eat the goose," Holmes said, smiling.

"You ate it!" the man exclaimed.

"It would have spoiled," Holmes said. "This other one," he pointed to the table, "is the same size and much fresher. Will it suit you?"

"Oh, yes," Mr. Baker said with relief.

"We still have the feathers, the legs, and so on from your bird if you wish to have them…"

The man laughed. "I have no use for such things," he said.

"Fine," Holmes said. "By the way, could you tell me where you got such a decent bird?"

"Of course – it's the Alpha Inn, near the Museum. We pay a small amount each week through the year, the owner buys the birds at a good rate, and we get them Christmas Eve."

With that, the man bowed to us both, thanked us again, and left with his hat on his head and the goose under his arm.

"So much for Mr. Henry Baker," Holmes said. "Now I think we might visit the owner of the Alpha Inn. What do you say, Watson?"

CHAPTER 3

A Goose Chase

In fifteen minutes we were at the Alpha Inn, a small restaurant in a slightly seedy part of the city. Holmes pushed open the door and ordered us something to drink.

"Is your hot cider as good as your geese?" he asked the ruddy-faced, white-aproned owner.

The owner looked surprised. "My geese?" he exclaimed.

"Yes. I was just speaking to a Mr. Henry Baker – one of your goose club members."

"Ah, I see. Those weren't our geese. I got 'em from the market in Covent Garden."

Holmes nodded. "Who do you buy from?"

"I always go to a chap named Breckinridge. Would you be thinking of joining the goose club, sir?"

"Thank you, no," Holmes said.

We soon set out again. This time we walked south and at last came to Covent Garden Market. One of the largest stalls had the name "Breckinridge" on it.

Holmes walked up to a horsey-faced man with a trim beard who seemed to be the owner.

"I see you're sold out of geese," Holmes said.

"You can buy some from over there," the man replied, pointing to another stall.

"I was told you sold the best," Holmes said.

"Who by?"

"The owner of the Alpha Inn. He says you sent him two dozen fine birds. Where'd you get the geese you sold him?" Holmes asked.

To our surprise the question seemed to anger the man.

"Now then, mister," he said with his hands on his hips. "What are you getting at? Let's have it straight."

"This is all straight enough. I just want to know who sold you the geese that you sold to the Alpha Inn."

"Well, I'm not going to tell you."

Holmes sighed, as if the matter was not important. "I wonder why you should be upset over such a small thing."

"Upset! You would be upset if you had been pestered as I am. People asking, 'Where are the geese?' and 'Who did you sell the geese to?' I'm sick of it."

Holmes smiled. "I have nothing to do with any of those people. I just bet a friend of mine that those geese were raised in the country."

The man sniffed. "Well, you will lose your money," he said. "They are town-bred."

"Impossible!" Holmes said. "You cannot fool me about such birds."

"Do you think you know more about them than I do? I've handled fowls since I was a lad!"

"Nonsense," Holmes said. "You are simply confused, that's all."

"Do you wanna bet?" the man asked.

Holmes held up a gold coin. "Certainly, but how can you prove it?"

The man chuckled. "Bring my book, Bill!"

A small boy brought a thin black book. The man opened it. "Now, Mr. Know-It-All, let us

see. Here we have all the records of what is bought and sold." He ran his finger down the page. "Why don't you read what it says there, sir." He pointed at an entry in the book.

"Oakshott, 117 Brixton Road," Holmes read.

"And on the facing page?" the man said with a smile.

"December 22nd. Twenty-four geese, paid in full on delivery."

"And next to that?"

"Sold to Mr. Windigate of the Alpha Inn. Ah, it looks as if he paid for them then."

"What do you have to say now?" the man asked with a smile of triumph.

Holmes shook his head and handed him the gold coin. He turned away as if he were too disappointed to speak. We had walked a few yards when he stopped and winked at me. "I know a betting man when I see one," he said.

"So are we going to Brixton Road now?" I asked. It was getting late and very cold, but I knew nothing would stop him.

Holmes was about to answer when there was a loud commotion from the stall behind us. Breckinridge was shouting at a small man with a sharp, pointed face.

"If you come around here pestering me any more, I will set the dog on you! Bring Mrs. Oakshott here and I'll talk to her. What is it with you? Did I buy the geese from you?"

"No, but one of those geese was mine," the man whined. "She told me to ask you."

"Well, you can ask the Queen of England for it for all I care. Get out of here!"

"This may save us a trip to Brixton Road," Holmes said. "Let us see what we can make of this fellow." He hurried after the small man who had asked the questions.

"Excuse me," Holmes said. "I heard you asking the salesman about geese. I think I may be able to help you."

"How do you know anything about it?" the man said suspiciously.

"My name is Sherlock Holmes and it is my business to know what other people do not know. You are trying to track down some geese sold by Mrs. Oakshott. Those geese were sold to Mr. Windigate of the Alpha Inn."

The man stretched out his hand. "You are the man I have longed to meet," he said.

"Indeed," Holmes said. "Then we had better discuss it in a warm room, not here in the street." He stopped a cab and we all got in. "May I know your name?"

"Er, it's... it's John Robinson."

"No, no," Holmes said sweetly, "your *real* name. It is hard doing business with an alias."

The man turned red. "James Ryder," he said.

"Exactly," Holmes said. "Aren't you the porter at the Hotel Cosmopolitan?"

Nothing more was said during the journey to Baker Street. Ryder looked as if he did not know what to make of things. Was this a stroke of good luck or bad?

CHAPTER 4

The Game Is Up

We entered Holmes' study, where the fire was still burning.

"You look cold," Holmes said. "Do sit near the fire. Now, you want to know what became of those geese? Or should I say one special goose. Perhaps a goose with a black bar of feathers across the tail?"

Ryder's eyes opened wide. "Can you tell me where that goose has gone?"

"It came here."

"Here?"

"Yes. What a very special bird it was. Do you know, it laid an egg after it was dead! A bright blue egg." Holmes opened his safe and took out the blue carbuncle, which shone like a star.

Ryder stood up. I thought he might fall over but he grabbed the table. He stared at the jewel.

"The game's up, Ryder," Holmes said. He turned to me. "Look at him, Watson. He hasn't the backbone for this sort of crime."

Indeed, the man was as white as a sheet. He sat staring at Holmes with his eyes full of fear.

"I know enough to put you behind bars," Holmes said coldly. "You may as well tell me the rest. You had heard of this jewel belonging to the Countess of Morcar?"

"Her maid, Catherine Cusack, told me."

"I see. Not a pretty crime, Ryder. You were happy to let Horner go to prison for it. You knew he had a prison record so you asked him to come and make a repair to the Countess's

room. You probably caused the damage yourself and he walked into you little trap."

Ryder fell on the rug and begged at Holmes's feet. "Have mercy!" he cried. "Think of my parents. It would break their hearts. I never went wrong before. I never will again!"

"Get back in your chair," Holmes said sternly. "It is all very well to whine now and beg now but you thought little enough of this poor Horner, who stands accused!"

"I'll leave the country! Without me, the case against him would collapse."

Holmes was silent. Then he said, "We shall see. Tell me how the jewel got into the goose. Tell me the truth, for it is your only hope."

Ryder started talking eagerly. "After Horner was arrested, I knew I had to hide the jewel. The police would search the hotel. So I went to my sister's house in Brixton Road. While we stood in the yard where the geese were, I was thinking how I could get the stone to someone I knew who could sell it.

"My sister had said I could have a goose for Christmas. As I looked at them I had the idea that would save me. No one would look for the jewel in a goose!

"When my sister went inside I caught the bird with that bar of black feathers on its tail. I pried its bill open and pushed in the jewel. It gave a gulp, and swallowed the thing.

"Just then my sister came out again. I let go of the bird and asked her if I could take my goose with me that day.

"Of course," she said. "Take your pick." So I caught the one with the barred tail, killed it, and took it to Kilburn.

"Then, when I opened up the goose I found nothing! My heart turned to water. I left it there and rushed back to my sister. The yard was empty! All the birds had gone. She told me they had all gone to the dealer in Covent Garden. 'Was there another one with a barred tail?' I asked. 'Yes,' she said, 'there were two barred-tailed ones. I never could tell them apart.' To top it off, that stupid man would never tell me where he had sold them.

"I tried again tonight. You heard me. My sister thinks I am crazy – I'm starting to think so myself. Now I am a thief and I have never had any gains from my crime. What am I to do?" He burst into sobs, his face in his hands.

There was a long silence. At last Holmes got up and went to the door. "Get out!" he said, opening it.

"Oh, sir. Thank you!"

"I don't want to hear it. Just be gone."

After he fled, Holmes turned to me and said, "I am not here to make up for what the police lack. If Ryder is sent to jail he'll be in and out of prison all his life. I don't think he'll go wrong again – he's had too much of a scare. Nor will he go to court against Horner. The case will collapse." He stretched out his long legs toward the fire. "Just think, Watson, we began with a hat and a goose! Chance placed in our way a most odd problem – and I think its solution is its own reward."

The Adventure of the Silver Blaze

CHAPTER 1

A Disappearance and a Death

"I am afraid, Watson, that I shall have to go," Holmes said, looking up from his newspaper.

"Go? Where to?" I asked.

"To Dartmoor. To King's Pyland."

I was not surprised. The disappearance of the horse called Silver Blaze was the big news story. Silver Blaze was the favorite to win the Wessex Cup, but the horse was missing and its trainer had been killed.

"I would be happy to go with you," I said, "as long as I'm not in the way."

"My dear Watson, you would do me a great favor. This looks like a unique case."

So it happened that an hour or so later we were on our way to King's Pyland, home of the famous stables. On the way, Holmes told me the details of the case.

"Silver Blaze has won many races for his owner, Colonel Ross. He was also the favorite to win the Wessex Cup. The horse is well liked by the public and a lot of money has been staked on him. It is clear, then, that many people had a strong interest in keeping Silver Blaze from racing."

"What about the trainer?"

"John Straker had been the trainer for seven years, and had a clean record. There were three stable lads. One of them sat up each night in the stable while the others slept up in the loft. According to my information, they are all reliable boys," Holmes said.

"What else do you know about Straker?"

"He was a married man without children, who lived in a small house near the stables. The country around is very lonely, but about half a mile north there is a group of houses. Across the moor, about two miles, are the Mapleton stables. They are owned by Lord Blackwater and managed by Silas Brown. In all other directions the moor is deserted apart from a few gypsies who roam the area."

"Tell me more," I said.

"On the evening in question, the horses were fed and watered as usual and the stables were locked at nine o'clock. Two of the lads went up to the trainer's house where they had supper. The other lad, Ned Hunter, was left on guard. Shortly after nine, the maid, Edith, took Ned a dish of curried lamb for his supper."

"What did the unfortunate boy drink?"

"There was a tap in the stable. It was a rule that the lad on duty must stick close and drink nothing else. Edith was a little way from the stables when she was stopped by a man. She said he was 'a gentleman' and wore a gray suit and a cloth cap. He carried a heavy stick and she noticed that his face was very pale and that he seemed nervous."

"Go on, Holmes. I haven't heard any of this."

"As usual, the newspapers only have room for *some* of the facts," Holmes said. "The man asked Edith where he was. She told him he was close to King's Pyland stables. 'What a stroke of luck,' he said. 'Now, would you like to earn a little extra money?' and he tried to give her a piece of paper to give to the stable boy.

"But Edith ran to the stable where Ned was already at the little table by the window. He looked up and she passed him his meal as normal. As she started to tell him what had happened, the stranger appeared again. 'Good evening,' he said to Ned, through the open window. 'I wanted to have a word with you.'

"'What do you want here?' asked the lad.

"'Just some information – which I will pay you for. Tell me, is it true that the horse Silver Blaze could beat the other horses hands down, even if they had a huge head start – and that the stables have bet their money on him?'

"'We don't talk about that with people like you!' the lad said. 'Get out of here now!' He went out to set the dog free. The girl ran off but she saw the stranger still leaning through the window. Then, when Ned came out of the stable with the dog, the man was gone."

"Did the stable boy leave the door unlocked behind him?" I asked with interest.

"Excellent, Watson," Holmes murmured. "I asked the same question. I was told that Ned locked the door."

"What about over the door?"

"He wouldn't have had time to climb over and back. Ned waited until the other lads came back and then he sent a message to the trainer. Straker was very uneasy. At one o'clock his wife woke up to find him dressing. He said he was going to see that all was well."

"Was that the last she saw of him?"

"The last she saw of him alive. At seven o'clock she woke and went down to the stables. Ned Hunter was fast asleep. The horse was missing and there was no sign of the trainer.

"She woke the lads in the loft but they had heard nothing. Ned, however, could not be roused and so they left him to sleep. The lads and the woman ran off to search.

"A short way off they found the body of the trainer. He had a dreadful head wound and a long cut in the thigh. He seemed to have put up a fight; his hand still held a small knife which had blood on it up to the handle. In his

left hand he held a red and black silk necktie, which the maid said she had seen the stranger wearing. When Ned recovered from his drugged sleep he also recognized the necktie."

"What about the horse?" I asked.

"There were signs that the horse had been at the scene of the murder. However, it has since been impossible to find it."

"How was the lad drugged?"

"Traces of a sleeping powder were found in the remains of his supper."

I whistled. "What about the stranger?"

"He has been found – and arrested by Inspector Gregory, who is in charge of the case.

The man's name is Fitzroy Simpson and he lived in one of the nearby houses. He has lost a fortune betting on horses and he now lives by placing bets for others and giving racing tips. He bet five thousand pounds against the favorite, Silver Blaze."

"Conclusive evidence, wouldn't you say? What was his story?"

"He admitted coming to get information about the horses at King's Pyland. He also wanted to find out about the horses at the other stables, such as at Mapleton. That is where the second favorite horse, Desborough, lives. He did not deny being at the stables but said he had no other plans."

"What about his necktie?"

"He could not explain how it came to be in the hand of the dead man. He also still had his walking stick, which could have been the weapon that killed Straker."

"Then there is no mystery?"

"He wasn't wounded – and Straker's knife shows that someone must have been injured."

"Could the blood on the knife be Straker's?"

"That is quite possible. The police believe that Simpson drugged the lad and kidnapped the horse. Perhaps Simpson had a copy of the key from somewhere. Silver Blaze's bridle is missing, so he must have put it on. Somewhere, the police think, he bumped into the trainer and a fight took place."

"And the horse bolted?" I suggested.

"Or was taken to a hiding place. Though how Simpson expected to get away with such a crime is, indeed, a mystery." At this point Holmes sank back into thought and remained quiet for the rest of the journey.

CHAPTER 2

On the Trail

When we arrived at the station, we met Colonel Ross and Inspector Gregory. Together we set off for King's Pyland.

"Thank you for coming, Mr. Holmes," the Colonel said. "I am determined to avenge poor Straker – and to recover my horse."

"The evidence against Simpson is very strong," the Inspector said calmly. "He had much to gain if Silver Blaze could not race. Things like the stick and necktie are very much against him."

Holmes shook his head. "A clever defense lawyer would tear it to shreds," he said. "Why take the horse? He could injure it where it was. Has a copy of the key been found? Where did he get the sleeping powder? Above all, where would he hide a horse?"

The Inspector nodded. He did not resent Holmes' objections and he took a while to reply. "A key could be thrown away on the moors. He could obtain the.powder at almost any pharmacy in London, where he came from, and the horse may well be at the bottom of one of the many pits or mines in the area."

"What does he say about the necktie?"

"He admits it's his and says that he lost it. There is one other clue, however. A party of gypsies were camped within a mile of the spot where Straker was found. The following day they had gone. Simpson could have easily passed the horse on to them. We are searching for them now."

"What about the other stables? The Mapleton stables?"

"We have been there. The Mapleton trainer, Silas Brown, certainly had large bets on the race; and he was no friend of Straker, but there is nothing to connect him with the crime."

"Is there nothing to connect Simpson with the interests of the Mapleton stables?"

"Nothing at all."

Holmes leaned back in the carriage and the conversation ceased.

When we stepped out of the carriage, I noticed that Holmes had a gleam in his eye. I knew he had already thought of something that the others had missed.

"I should like to see what Straker had with him at the time of his death," he said.

The Inspector nodded amiably and led him into the house. On a table was a small heap of things: a box of matches, a piece of candle, a pipe, a tobacco pouch, a silver watch with a gold chain, five gold coins, a pencil case, a few papers, and a small knife with a blade marked "Weiss & Co." It was still stained with blood.

"This is a very special knife," said Holmes. "This is in your line, Watson."

"Yes," I said. "It is a cataract knife. It has a very delicate blade for very delicate work."

"It's a strange thing for a man to carry on a rough night," Holmes said.

"His wife told us it was on the dressing table before he went out," the Inspector said. "It had a cork to guard the tip. Perhaps it was the best weapon he could think of as he left the house."

"The papers are of interest," Holmes said, turning over a pile of documents. "Look at this bill from an expensive dress shop, made out to William Darbyshire. This Darbyshire was a friend of Straker's, according to his wife."

"Someone has expensive tastes," I smiled.

As we left, a pale and haggard woman stopped us. "What have you found?" she asked.

Holmes did not answer her directly. Smiling gently, he said, "Haven't we met?"

The woman shook her head.

"Weren't you dressed in dove-colored silk dress with ostrich feather trim?"

"You are mistaken. I never had such a dress," the woman said hastily.

Holmes apologized and we walked outside.

A short stroll took us to the murder scene, where Holmes bent to examine the ground. He took a long time and the Colonel became impatient, often looking at his watch while Holmes continued his systematic search.

"Ah-ha!" Holmes said at last, and picked up a half-burnt match. He then compared the prints in the mud with a boot of John Straker's and one of Silver Blaze's horseshoes.

Finally he turned back to the Colonel. "Now, if you will excuse us, Watson and I will take a little walk over the moors. I shall put the horseshoe in my pocket for luck."

As we walked away, in the direction of Mapleton, he said, "Where is the horse? Let us imagine what might happen to it. Would it run loose for long? No. Horses seek company. Kidnapped by gypsies? They would never be able to sell a horse like that. A loose horse would head for Mapleton or King's Pyland. It is not at King's Pyland. Therefore it must be at Mapleton."

We soon came to a dip in the land and Holmes stopped. "This must have been wet on Monday. Let us see if there are tracks here."

He soon shouted. I ran over and found him fitting the horseshoe into a mark in the mud. "Such is the value of imagination, Watson. It is the one thing Inspector Gregory lacks."

As we got closer to Mapleton, we saw the marks of the horse once more, this time with a man's tracks beside them. Suddenly they changed direction again, toward King's Pyland. Holmes whistled. Then I spotted the same tracks, returning toward Mapleton.

"Well done," Holmes said. "You saved us another long walk, Watson."

As we approached Mapleton stables, a groom ran out and asked what we wanted.

"If I were here at five o'clock tomorrow morning to see your employer, Silas Brown, would I be too early?" Holmes asked genially.

"No, sir. He is always the first one up and about, but here he comes now!"

An annoyed-looking gentleman came through the gate. "What do you want here?"

"All I need is ten minutes of your time," said Holmes calmly.

"I've no time for gossiping," the man said. He turned as if to go, but Holmes stepped forward, laid a hand on his arm, and whispered in his ear. Immediately Brown's face reddened with fury.

"It's a lie!" he cried. "An infernal lie!"

"Very well," Holmes said. "Shall we argue about it in public or indoors?"

"Oh, come in, if you must," the man said.

CHAPTER 3

A Horse Is Found

I waited for twenty minutes. At last, Holmes and the trainer came out. Silas Brown's face was now gray and he was covered in sweat.

"It will be done as you say," was all he said.

"There must be no mistake." There was menace in Holmes's voice as he walked away.

After a little distance, he said, "What a coward. He tried to deny it but I described so exactly what had happened that he thought I had seen him."

"What did you say?" I asked, amazed.

"I said that early in the morning, he saw a strange horse wandering nearby. When he got closer he realized it was Silver Blaze. He started to lead it back to King's Pyland – but then thought that if he hid Silver Blaze until after the race, his horse would almost certainly win!"

"But the stables have been searched," I said.

"An old horse-faker like him has many a trick. So now we must return to London."

"To London? What about Straker's killer?"

"All in good time, Watson."

The Colonel sneered when Holmes told him he was leaving. "So we are no farther forward than when you arrived?"

"We shall see," said Holmes. "But I promise your horse will run in the Wessex Cup."

"I'd rather have my horse than your promise," the Colonel said.

Holmes looked at him coldly. Then, as we left, Holmes spoke to a stable lad. "You have a few sheep here. Who looks after them?"

"I do, sir."

"Has anything happened to them lately?"

"Well, three have gone lame this week."

Holmes grinned. "A long shot, Watson! Remember that point, Inspector."

"Anything else?" Inspector Gregory asked.

"Yes, the dog's strange behavior that night."

"But the dog did nothing."

"That was the strange behavior."

CHAPTER 4

The Wessex Cup

Four days later, Holmes and I set off to see the Wessex Cup. Colonel Ross met us at the racecourse. His manner was cold.

"I have seen nothing of my horse," he said.

"Would you know him?" Holmes asked.

"Of course!" Ross said angrily. "You can't miss the white blaze on his head and the white mark on his foreleg! Do you think I'm a fool?"

Holmes did not reply. "I understand Silver Blaze is still favorite," was all he would say.

"There are six in the race," I said, "and there are six horses ready to run down there."

"I still don't see him!" the Colonel cried.

"Let us just see how they run," Holmes replied with a confident smile.

To begin with, the horses were all close together. Then Desborough, the Mapleton horse, took the lead. However, twenty yards from the winning post, a big bay horse swept into the lead and won easily by six lengths.

"We need to go to the winners' enclosure," Holmes said and led the way.

Once inside, he turned to the Colonel. "Here is your horse. Just wash his face and his leg in rubbing alcohol and you will recognize Silver Blaze."

"My horse! But how...?"

"I found him in the hands of a gentleman who is well-versed in such things. To him it was an easy matter to hide Silver Blaze's white markings. He was put in the race just as he looked when he arrived."

The Colonel shook his head. "You have done wonders and I owe you an apology. You found my horse. If only you could find the killer of John Straker."

"I have done so. He is here," Holmes said.

The Colonel looked angry again.

Then Holmes said, "The murderer is behind you." He put his hand on the neck of the horse. "It was self-defense!"

CHAPTER 5

Holmes Explains

Later Holmes explained. "It was the curried mutton, the only dish which would hide the taste of the bitter sleeping powder. How could Simpson have known that Ned's food that night would be curry? That's when my suspicion fell on Straker and his wife. They were the only ones who could control the food."

He continued, "Then there was the dog that did not bark when a stranger came in the night! The stable lads in the loft would have heard it bark but it was silent. It would only be silent if it knew the person who came in."

"So why would Straker want to steal his own horse?" I asked, still mystified.

"To injure it so it could not race, because he had money on the second favorite. He had to do it in a way that would not be noticed.

Remember the delicate knife? Straker planned to use it to nick the tendons of the horse's leg to make the horse lame."

"The scoundrel!" the Colonel cried.

"Straker had to do this somewhere quiet so he took the horse onto the moors. He needed the candle in order to see what he was doing..."

"And you found the match!" I said. "What drove him to this?"

"A woman, my dear Watson. You remember the bill? Men do not carry other people's bills. Straker was also Mr. Darbyshire."

"And he was buying expensive dresses for another woman?"

"That was easy to discover. Remember that I found out from Mrs. Straker that she had never

had such a dress. The shop's address was on the bill. So we returned to London and they recognized the photograph of Straker."

"What about the necktie?"

"Simpson dropped it in his hurry to get away. Straker saw it and maybe hoped it would be useful for tying the horse's leg. He took the horse to the hollow and tried to carry out his plan but he had not reckoned on the horse. It lashed out and its hoof struck Straker on the head. He fell and the knife cut his leg."

"What about the sheep?" I asked, remembering Holmes' questioning of the lad.

"That was a long shot! I thought a man like Straker would take care to practice – and where better than on a sheep or two? They were the desperate actions of a desperate man," Holmes said.

"Where *was* the horse?" the Colonel asked.

"Ahem," Holmes said. "It bolted... and was cared for by a horse-lover, shall we say. I think the less said about that, the better. Shall we go and inspect the horses in last race of the day?"

The Adventure of the Copper Beeches

CHAPTER 1

A Dangerous Offer

It was a cold morning in early spring. Holmes and I were sitting on each side of a cheery fire in the study in Baker Street. Holmes puffed irritably on his pipe.

"Crime is common. Logic is rare," he said, "and who cares for logic anymore? My work seems to be nothing more than an agency for recovering lost pencils and giving advice to young ladies from boarding schools."

I stayed silent. Holmes was best left alone when he was in this mood.

"This note," he continued, "marks the lowest point of my career. Read it!"

He tossed a crumpled letter to me. It said:

Dear Mr. Holmes,

I am very anxious to consult you as to whether I should or should not accept a post as governess. I shall call at half-past ten tomorrow if that is convenient for you.

Yours faithfully,

Violet Hunter

At that moment the bell rang and shortly after, a young woman, plainly but neatly dressed, entered the room. She had a bright face and a brisk, businesslike manner.

"I am sorry to trouble you," she said, "but I have had a very strange experience. I have no parents or anyone else to ask for advice."

"Do take a seat, Miss Hunter," Holmes said kindly. "I shall be happy to help you if I can."

Miss Hunter began. "I have been a governess for five years. Two months ago my employer went to Canada and I found myself without a job. I use an agency in London and I call once a week to see if there's a job to suit me. You will understand that I have very few savings and I need to find a post very soon.

"Last week when I called, Miss Stoper, the agency owner, was not alone in her office. There was a man with her – a very stout man with a smiling, ruddy face.

"When I went in he said, 'That will do! I could not ask for better!' Then he spoke to me with a most engaging smile. 'What salary do you ask?'

"'Four pounds a month.'

"'Pitiful!' he cried. 'Your salary with me would start at a hundred pounds a year.'

"This seemed too good to be true. I felt that I needed to know more so I asked, 'May I enquire where you live, sir?'

"'Hampshire. A place called Copper Beeches near Winchester. You would care for one child of six, that's all. You should see him killing cockroaches with a slipper! Smack, smack!'

"'My only duties are to look after the one child?' I asked, wanting to be sure.

"'Your duty would be to obey any little commands that my wife might give. Nothing out of the ordinary, I assure you.'

"'I should be happy to make myself useful.'

"'Quite so. Now… about the matter of dress. We are faddy people – but kind. If we asked you to wear a special dress, for example, would you object?'

"'No,' I said, though I was surprised.

"'Would you cut your hair short?'

"I could hardly believe my ears. My hair is my pride and joy.

"'Oh,' I said, without thinking what I was saying, 'I'm afraid that is impossible.'

"'But it must be done,' the man said. 'My wife has these fancies and you know how such fancies must be obeyed…'

"'I'm sorry,' I said. 'It really is impossible.'

"His smile disappeared and he looked disappointed. 'What a shame. In all other ways you are quite perfect.'

"The agency owner looked both upset and cross. As I left the room I thought that it would now be highly unlikely for me to get a job through her agency. When I got home and saw more bills to be paid, I decided I had been foolish. I had lost a good job just by refusing to cut my hair!

"The next day, however, there was a letter from the man, who is named Jephro Rucastle. He offered to raise the salary to £120 a year and asked me again to take the position."

She passed the letter to Sherlock Holmes. He read it with interest.

"Should I take the job, Mr. Holmes?"

Holmes sighed. "I think you've already decided."

"Should I refuse? I do need the money and the salary is good."

"It is too good. Why should he pay £120 when he could get someone for £40? I would not like a sister of mine to take such a job."

She looked downcast. "I thought if I told you all about it – I might be able to ask your help if I needed it."

"You may rely on my support. If you find yourself in danger…"

"Danger!" she cried. "What danger do you foresee?"

"It would cease to be a danger if we knew what it was. Send me a telegram any time, day or night, and we shall be there."

Violet stood up. "Thank you. Tonight I shall cut my hair and tomorrow I shall go down to Copper Beeches easy in my mind." She thanked us again and left.

"We will hear from her before many days have passed," Holmes said. He sighed – but he already seemed to be more cheerful.

CHAPTER 2

A Telegram Arrives

Holmes' words turned out to be correct. Two weeks later a telegram came.

Please be at the Black Swan Hotel in Winchester at midday tomorrow. Do come. I am at my wit's end. Violet Hunter.

The following morning we were on our way.

"The countryside seems such a peaceful place," Holmes said as he looked out of the train window. "But think of what can go on in the deserted houses and hamlets. In the country, there is no one to report the evil that may be taking place."

His words were chilling and I was glad to see Violet Hunter safe at the Black Swan when we arrived.

"I am so delighted that you have come," she said earnestly.

We sat in a quiet corner, "Let us have everything in its due order," Holmes said, thrusting his long thin legs out toward the fire and closing his eyes to listen.

Violet began her story.

CHAPTER 3

Violet's Story

I have had no ill-treatment but I cannot understand Mr. and Mrs. Rucastle. I must say I am not easy in my mind about them.

When I came here, Mr. Rucastle met me at the train and drove me to the house. It is in a pretty area but the house itself is not beautiful. It was once white but is now badly weathered. In front of the house are the copper beeches that give it its name.

Mrs. Rucastle is a silent, pale woman, much younger than her husband. He is a widower and already has a grown-up daughter, who, I was told, had gone to America.

Mr. Rucastle married again and now has a son of six: a spoiled, ill-natured boy who seems to enjoy giving pain to anything weaker than himself.

Then there are the servants, Mr. and Mrs. Toller. Mr. Toller is a rough, uncouth man with grizzled hair and whiskers. He smells and is hopelessly irresponsible, though Mr. Rucastle seems to take no notice.

Mrs. Toller is tall and strong. She has a sour face and is as silent as Mrs. Rucastle. They are a very unpleasant couple.

The first day I was there, Mr. Rucastle took me to an outbuilding and showed me a huge animal. "This is Carlo, my hound," he said. "Toller is the only one who can control him. We let him loose at night. Do not ever set foot outside at night! Your life would be in danger!"

The sight of that dreadful animal sent a chill to my heart.

On the third day Mr. Rucastle called me to his study. "Thank you for pleasing us by cutting your hair," he said. "I wonder if you would put on the dress that is on your bed, then come to the drawing room."

The dress that I found in my room was an unusual blue. It had been worn before but it fitted me very well. When I entered the drawing room, Mr. and Mrs. Rucastle were very pleased and said how much it suited me.

They asked me to sit close to the long window, which I did. The chair faced away from the window, so I could not see out. Mr. Rucastle walked up and down telling me stories. He was a good teller of very funny stories and I laughed a lot, but Mrs. Rucastle just sat there and looked sad.

Two days later I was asked to do the same thing. Again I changed my dress and sat in the window, and again Mr. Rucastle told stories.

I was very curious and wanted to see what was going on behind my back. The next time I hid a small hand mirror in my handkerchief. I pretended I was wiping my eyes from laughing so much but, using it, I managed to see out onto the road. There was a man looking up at the window.

I think Mrs. Rucastle saw what I was doing. She stood up. "Jephro," she said, "there is a man on the road staring at Miss Hunter."

"Dear me. How rude of him. Please, Miss Hunter, turn around and wave him away."

I did as I was told. Mr. Rucastle then pulled down the blind. I was not asked to sit near the window again, nor was I asked to wear the blue dress anymore.

After a few days I had a good idea of the layout of the house. There was one wing where no one seemed to live. The door to that part of the house was always locked. When I looked at that wing from the outside, I saw that there were four windows in a row. Three of them looked dirty but the other one had shutters that were closed.

When I asked Mr. Rucastle about it, he looked startled. "Photography is one of my hobbies," he said. "I have a darkroom there.

What a clever young lady you are to notice such things." He spoke in a joking tone but I think he was annoyed.

I was very curious and I also had a feeling that I ought to find out more. Yesterday my chance came. Toller was asleep in front of the fire in the kitchen. He had left a key in the door to the hidden part of the house so I was able to open the door and slip through.

In front of me was a little passage, off which I could see several doors. They were all open except one, under which there was a light showing. It was fastened with a huge padlock. I stood gazing at the sinister door and wondering what was behind it. Then I heard steps inside the room. Suddenly I felt very scared and I turned and ran back down the passage, clutching at the skirt of my dress.

As I rushed through the door, I ran straight into Mr. Rucastle.

"So!" he said. "What have you been up to? What has frightened you?" he asked quietly. His voice was coaxing – but I felt I needed to be careful of what I said.

"I was foolish enough to go into the empty wing, but it is so lonely and still in there, I suddenly felt scared."

He looked at me and his eyes became hard and fierce. "Now you know why I keep it locked. Miss Hunter, if I find you there again... I shall throw you to the hound!"

CHAPTER 4

The Rescue

"I ran to my room," Violet continued. "Everything seemed horrible: the house, the servants, the Rucastles – even the child. I used my afternoon off to walk into the village and send the telegram. This morning I slipped out of the house while the Rucastles were out. Toller was not around and Mrs. Toller was in the kitchen garden." She paused and looked at Holmes. "I am so glad to see you here. I know there is something wrong but I cannot figure out what it might be."

"We shall soon unravel this," Holmes said, rising and pacing up and down the room. "Is there a cellar with a strong lock?"

"Why, yes," she said, "the wine cellar."

"You have been both brave and sensible. Can you do one more thing before we arrive?"

"I will try."

"Get Mrs. Toller to go to the cellar for some reason. Close and lock the door."

"I will do it!"

"Excellent. You are quite an exceptional woman. We shall follow in forty minutes. The only explanation is that you have been brought to Copper Beeches to impersonate someone. That person must be the daughter, Alice Rucastle. I fear that she is locked in the room that you discovered."

"How dreadful! Why?" Violet asked.

"The man in the road – the one you saw in your mirror – must be her sweetheart, perhaps her fiancé. You were brought there to show that Alice was alive and happy. You even waved him away, which they hoped would be enough to convince him that Alice no longer wished to see him."

"Why would they go to such extremes?"

"That," Holmes said in a determined voice, "is what we are here to find out."

Forty minutes later we arrived at Copper Beeches. Violet Hunter was waiting on the steps as we approached. "Have you managed it?" Holmes asked.

A loud thudding came from somewhere downstairs. "That is Mrs. Toller in the cellar," Violet said. "Her husband is snoring on the kitchen rug. Here are his keys."

"You have done well indeed!" Holmes cried with enthusiasm. "Now lead us to the room."

We went up the stairs, unlocked the door and walked down the passage. We came to the padlocked door. "Try your shoulder against it, Watson," Holmes said.

The door gave way easily and together we entered the room. It was empty. All we saw was a simple bed, a small table, and a basket of clothes.

"Look!" Violet said.

Above, in the ceiling, was a skylight. It was open. The prisoner was gone.

With my help, Holmes made his way up through the skylight. "Yes," he called, "there is a ladder over there." He dropped back into the room. "Someone is coming," he whispered. "Watson, have your pistol ready."

A fat, burly man appeared in the doorway with a heavy stick in his hand. Violet screamed and held on to my arm. Holmes strode up to him. "You villain. Where is your daughter?"

Rucastle's eyes were wide. He looked around and then saw the open skylight. "It is for you to tell me that! You thieves! Just wait!" He ran off down the passage.

"He's gone for the hound!" Violet cried.

"I have my revolver," I said.

We rushed along the passage and down the stairs. We reached the hall. Suddenly we heard a dreadful barking noise. Then there was a scream of agony. An old man with a red face and shaking limbs staggered into the room. It was Toller.

"Help me!" he cried. "Someone has let the dog loose. It has not been fed for two days. Quick, or it will be too late!"

We rushed out and around the side of the house. There we saw the huge hungry brute, its black muzzle buried in Rucastle's throat. The man writhed and screamed on the ground. I ran closer and shot it. As it fell over, its teeth were still locked onto Rucastle's neck.

The facts of the case were finally put together from Toller and his wife. Holmes explained on the train back to London.

"Alice Rucastle had money of her own but was happy to let her father handle her affairs. All was well until Alice fell in love with a naval officer. Rucastle knew that if she married, he would lose Alice's money."

"Is that why he locked her in the east wing and employed Violet – to get rid of him?"

"Exactly. It was an extreme plan – but Rucastle is an extreme man, with a cruel temper like his son. The seaman, however, did not go away. He too figured out what was going on. He bribed Mr. and Mrs. Toller. Then he brought the ladder and…"

"Rescued the damsel in distress. Just like in the fairy tale."

"Exactly, Watson. It was good that we were on hand when Rucastle returned. Who can tell what he would have done to Miss Hunter when he found that Alice was gone!"

Rucastle lived but he was from then on an invalid, kept alive by his devoted, sad wife. Alice Rucastle and her sailor were married. Violet Hunter is now the head of a school in Walsall, where I believe she has made a most successful career.

About the Author

Arthur Conan Doyle
1859 – 1930

Arthur Conan Doyle was trained as a doctor, but he always wanted to be a writer. He wrote his first Sherlock Holmes story in 1887, and it was a huge success. His readers demanded more stories.

By 1893, the writer had decided that he didn't want to be known only as "the Holmes man," so he wrote a story in which Holmes died. When it was published, some people in London wore black clothes, as if a relative of theirs had died! They also never stopped asking for more Holmes stories, so Conan Doyle had to bring his detective back to life.